For Toby and Martha

First published 2016 by Walker Books Ltd
87 Vauxhall Walk, London SE11 5HJ

This edition published 2017

2 4 6 8 10 9 7 5 3 1

This book has been typeset in Plantin

Printed in China

British Library Cataloguing in Publication Data:
a catalogue record for this book is available from the British Library

ISBN 978-1-4063-7383-7

www.walker.co.uk

WALKER BOOKS
AND SUBSIDIARIES
LONDON • BOSTON • SYDNEY • AUCKLAND

WILLY AND THE CLOUD

ANTHONY BROWNE

It all began on a warm, sunny day when Willy
decided to go to the park.
There wasn't a cloud in the sky when he set off.
(Well, just a little, tiny one.)

That's a bit annoying, he thought.

The cloud seemed to be following him.

What's going on?

I think it's gone...

Yes, it has gone. Phew!

(But Willy was wrong...)

At the park everyone seemed to be having great fun.

Willy just shivered.

So he went home.

Why was the cloud following him? What could he do?

"Hello," said Willy. "Is that the police?"

"Yes, sir. How can I help?"

"W-well, you see, I'm – I'm being followed."

"I see, sir. Who by? Can you give me a description?"

"Er … well, that's a bit difficult. It's – it's a cloud."

"You're being followed by a CLOUD, sir?"

"Yes – a BIG cloud…"

Willy heard the horrible sound of laughing policemen.

"Oh, dear," he said and put down the phone.

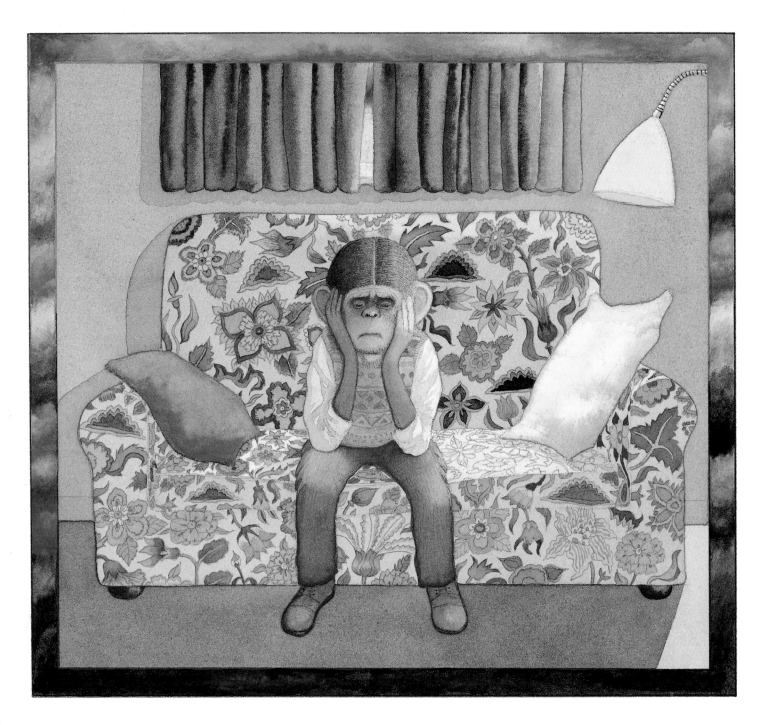

This cloud is awful, thought Willy. *How can I get rid of it?*
The room was getting darker and darker, so he turned on the
light and closed the curtains.

After a couple of hours Willy nervously peeped out of the window.
"Fantastic – it's gone!" he shouted.

(But he was wrong…)

Willy felt miserable. The house was becoming very hot.
He could hardly breathe. There seemed to be no air. He
heard loud, rumbling noises outside and slowly he began to
feel angry. Eventually he could stand it no longer.
He rushed outside…

Everything went quiet. What was happening?
Was the cloud crying? It felt rather wonderful.
The soft, cool rain was delicious.
Willy felt like singing … and even dancing!

After a while the rain stopped and the sun came out.

I think I'll try the park again, thought Willy.

And this time, when he got there
EVERYONE was happy!

Anthony Browne

Anthony Browne is one of the most celebrated author-illustrators of his generation. Acclaimed Children's Laureate from 2009 to 2011 and winner of multiple awards – including the prestigious Kate Greenaway Medal and the much coveted Hans Christian Andersen Award – Anthony is renowned for his unique style. His work is loved around the world.

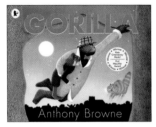

ISBN 978-1-4063-5233-7

ISBN 978-1-84428-559-4

ISBN 978-1-4063-1328-4

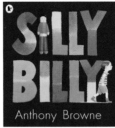
ISBN 978-1-4063-0576-0

ISBN 978-1-4063-1329-1

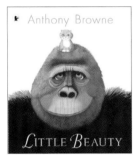
ISBN 978-1-4063-1930-9

ISBN 978-1-4063-1852-4

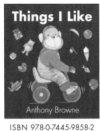
ISBN 978-0-7445-9858-2
ISBN 978-1-4063-2187-6
Board book edition

ISBN 978-1-4063-3851-5
ISBN 978-1-4063-4791-3
Board book edition

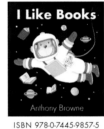
ISBN 978-0-7445-9857-5
ISBN 978-1-4063-2178-4
Board book edition

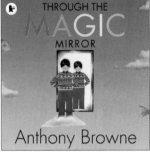
ISBN 978-1-4063-2628-4

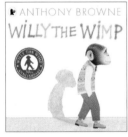
ISBN 978-1-4063-5641-0

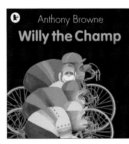
ISBN 978-1-4063-1873-9

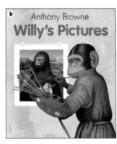
ISBN 978-1-4063-1356-7

ISBN 978-1-4063-1357-4

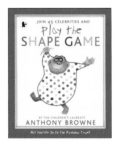
ISBN 978-1-4063-3131-8

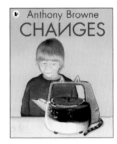
ISBN 978-1-4063-1339-0

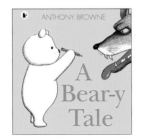
ISBN 978-1-4063-4162-1

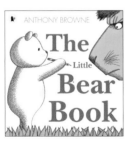
ISBN 978-1-4063-4163-8

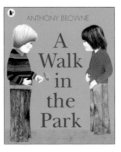
ISBN 978-1-4063-4164-5

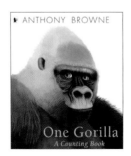
ISBN 978-1-4063-4533-9

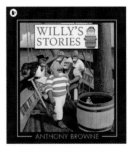
ISBN 978-1-4063-6089-9

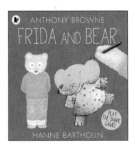
ISBN 978-1-4063-6557-3

Available from all good booksellers

www.walker.co.uk